Where's the
LLAMA?

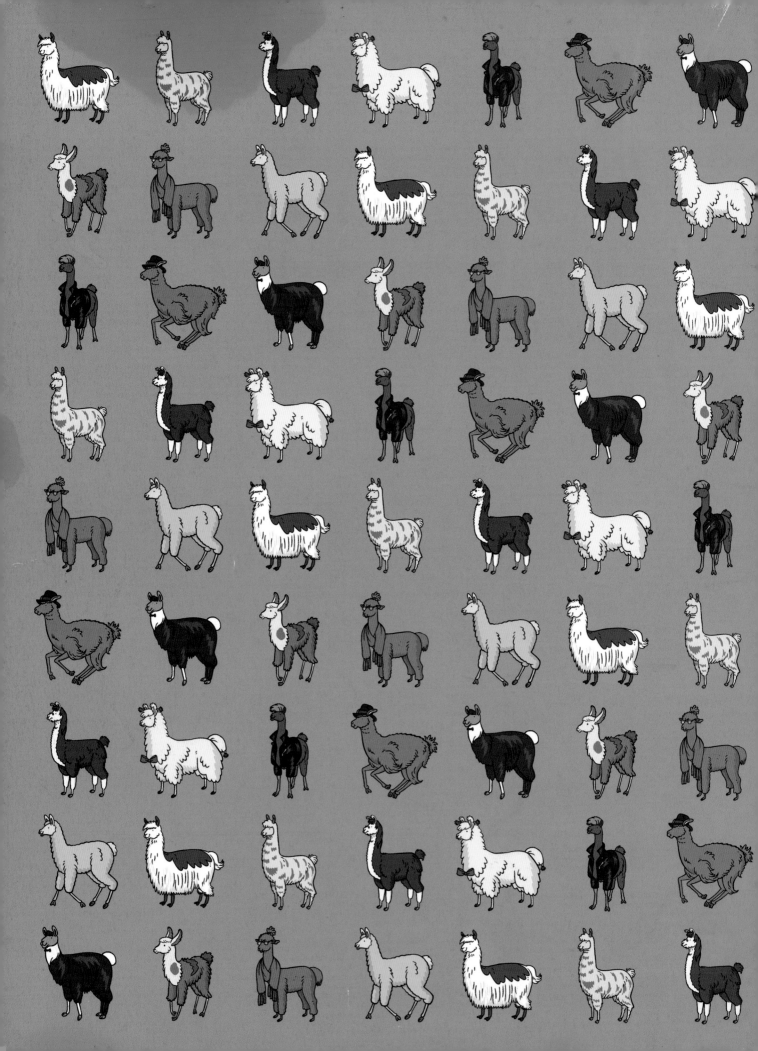

Where's the LLAMA?

ILLUSTRATED BY
PAUL MORAN

ADDITIONAL ARTWORK BY GERGELY FŐRIZS,
JORGE SANTILLAN, ADAM LINLEY,
AND JOHN BATTEN

WRITTEN BY FRANCES EVANS

Andrews McMeel
PUBLISHING®

INTRODUCTION

High up in the Peruvian Andes, a group of llamas have heard that the world is going crazy over . . . well . . . llamas! They can't help feeling flattered by this news, and being curious creatures, they've decided to embark on an incredible adventure to see the world and meet their adoring fans.

Head-llama Beatriz has planned an amazing trip that will take the herd to all kinds of exciting places—from a sunny Miami beach and a chic fashion show in Milan to an Indian palace and an ancient temple in Cambodia. With their bags packed and their guidebooks at the ready, the herd sets off for the airport.

Can you find all ten llamas in every scene? They are doing their best to blend in, so you'll need to keep your eyes peeled. You can find the answers, plus extra things to spot, at the back of the book.

BEATRIZ

Beatriz is the leader of the group. When she's not organizing the llamas' tour schedule, she's looking forward to relaxing in an Icelandic hot spring.

EDUARDO

In his youth, Eduardo was the first llama to fly around the world in a hot-air balloon. He's hoping to hook up with some old friends at a balloon festival in Japan.

ROSA

Adventurous Rosa loves being outdoors and can't wait to see the plants and wildlife in other countries. High on her bucket list is a trip to a tulip garden in the Netherlands.

LUIS

Dapper Luis is a bit of a foodie. He loves preparing exotic meals for the llamas and is desperate to sample the local delicacies in India, Mexico, and China.

ELENA

Elena's excited to soak up as much culture as she can on the trip. Her perfect day would involve browsing for bargains at a street market before swinging by a trendy art gallery.

CARLOS

Ever since he was a little cria (that's the word for a baby llama), Carlos has dreamed of trekking through the Cambodian jungle. He can't wait to explore its ancient temples.

DAPHNE

Glamorous Daphne has a passion for fashion—check out her earrings! She's hoping to wangle some tickets to a swanky catwalk show while the llamas are on tour.

RICARDO

Ricardo's a super-cool rock-and-roll llama. His perfect vacation would involve dancing all night long at the world's largest, grooviest music festival.

NELLY

When Nelly's not bouncing around the Andes, she's practicing her long-jump skills. She's hoping the llamas might get the chance to go to the Olympic Games.

HECTOR

Mischievous Hector is the cria of the group and will be keeping the other llamas on their toes during the trip. He's particularly excited about visiting a world-famous toy shop.

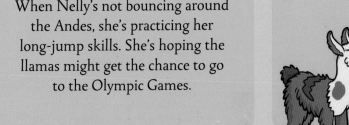

DAY OF THE DEAD

Beatriz has decided to kick off the tour in Mexico so the herd can take part in the annual Day of the Dead celebrations, or *Día de los Muertos* if you speak Spanish like the llamas do. They've arrived just in time to see an incredible street parade. The whole city has dressed up to honor their ancestors, and the costumes and giant floats look amazing.

Luis's guidebook recommends some sweets called *calaveras*—colorful sugar skulls—so the llamas set off into the crowd to find some.

Can you spot all ten llamas?

MIAMI BEACH

Next stop is Miami, Florida. The llamas have decided to make the most of the sun and sea by hitting the beach.

It's completely packed, so Daphne and Luis head into the crowd to find a spot for their towels, while Rosa and Hector join the line for ice cream. Ricardo is keen to rent a board and join the surfers on the waves, but the llamas don't often venture down to the coast, and he's a bit nervous of the water. He's going to dip a toe in first. . . .

Can you spot all ten llamas?

MODERN ART GALLERY

Elena's discovered that an award-winning artist has created a painting in honor of the herd. The llamas decide to swing by the gallery in New York to see the masterpiece and soak up a bit of culture.

Rosa is enjoying the abstract painting, and Carlos has discovered a passion for bronze sculptures. Beatriz and Eduardo aren't sure what to make of some of the more unusual objects on display, though.

Can you spot all ten llamas?

FAIRGROUND

The llamas have never been to a fairground before, so they're excited to try out all the rides at this amusement park in Ottawa, Canada.

Eduardo wants to go on the merry-go-round, while Beatriz and Elena have agreed to take Hector for a nail-biting ride on the flying swings. Rosa's found out she's a mean shot at the coconut tossing game, and Nelly's discovered an amazing thing called cotton candy. It looks a bit like pink llama wool! She's got to find the others to tell them about it.

Can you spot all ten llamas?

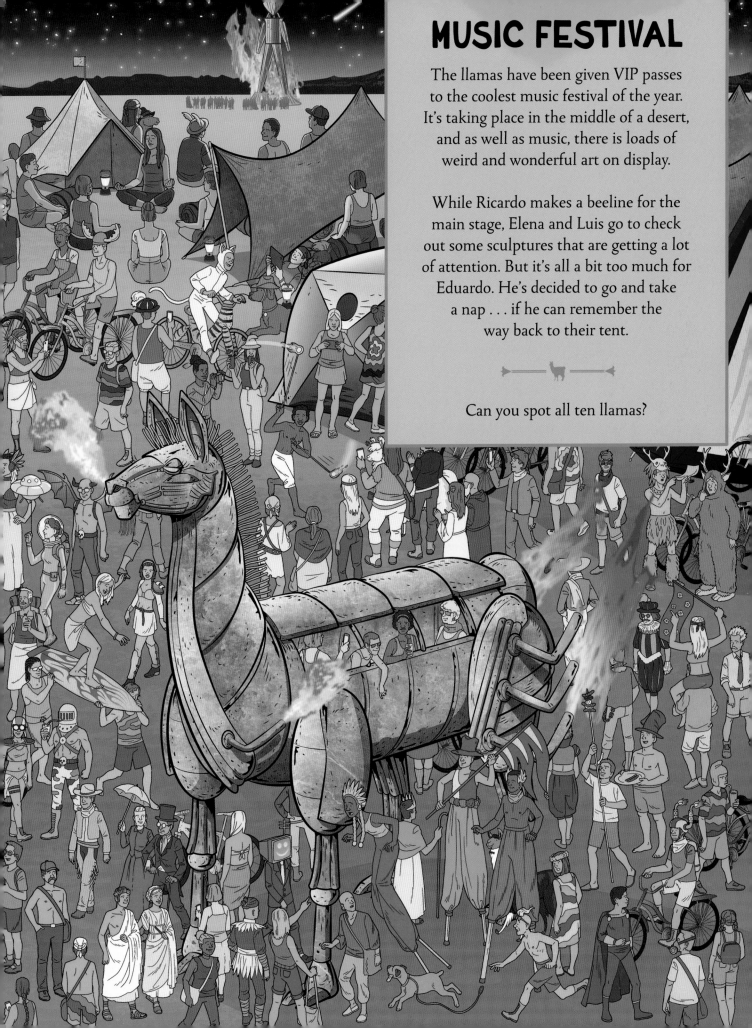

MUSIC FESTIVAL

The llamas have been given VIP passes to the coolest music festival of the year. It's taking place in the middle of a desert, and as well as music, there is loads of weird and wonderful art on display.

While Ricardo makes a beeline for the main stage, Elena and Luis go to check out some sculptures that are getting a lot of attention. But it's all a bit too much for Eduardo. He's decided to go and take a nap . . . if he can remember the way back to their tent.

Can you spot all ten llamas?

TULIP GARDEN

After a crazy weekend at the festival, the llamas have caught a plane to the Netherlands. They're spending an afternoon in a beautiful tulip garden.

The spring flowers here are completely different to those in Peru. Plant-mad Rosa is really excited—she's spotted a rare variety of tulip and has gone to investigate. Daphne and Eduardo want to splash through the stream, and Beatriz and Ricardo are going to admire the scene from a shady spot under the trees.

Can you spot all ten llamas?

STREET MARKET

On a weekend visit to Berlin, Germany, Elena persuades the herd to head downtown to a trendy street market. It's packed with people hunting for bargains, quirky accessories, and loads of delicious food. The llamas decide it's the perfect place to pick up some unique souvenirs.

Eduardo wants to buy a vintage travel map, and Daphne's gone in search of a popular cake stand. She's heard that it sells some adorable llama-shaped pastries!

Can you spot all ten llamas?

FASHION SHOW

The llamas have scored some tickets to a glamorous fashion show in Milan, Italy. Daphne is SO excited—she can't wait to get a sneak peek at next season's trends. She and Ricardo head backstage for some pampering, and a hairstylist suggests a shampoo that's just *perfect* for their woolly fleeces.

Luis goes to bag some seats in the front row, but Beatriz gets swept up in the crowd and starts accidentally photobombing the models. And . . . wait . . . is that Hector on the catwalk?

Can you spot all ten llamas?

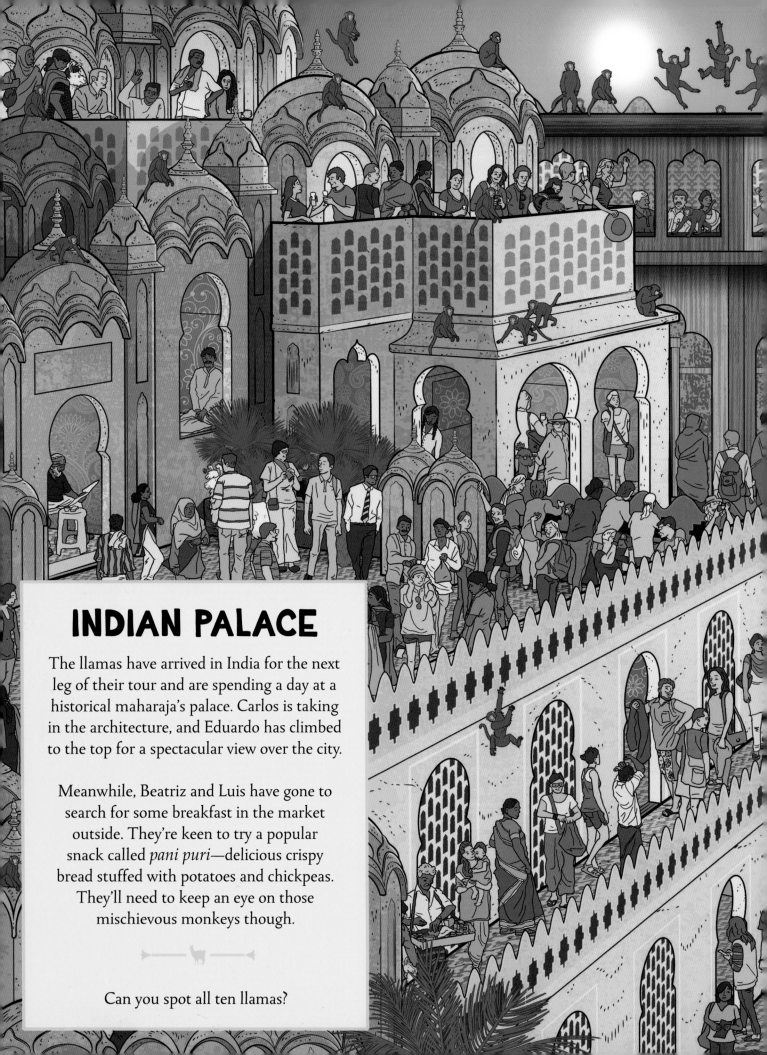

INDIAN PALACE

The llamas have arrived in India for the next leg of their tour and are spending a day at a historical maharaja's palace. Carlos is taking in the architecture, and Eduardo has climbed to the top for a spectacular view over the city.

Meanwhile, Beatriz and Luis have gone to search for some breakfast in the market outside. They're keen to try a popular snack called *pani puri*—delicious crispy bread stuffed with potatoes and chickpeas. They'll need to keep an eye on those mischievous monkeys though.

Can you spot all ten llamas?

CAMBODIAN JUNGLE

Carlos's dream has come true! Today, he is guiding the llamas through the rainforest to visit an ancient temple.

These magical ruins have been hidden from the outside world for centuries and are incredibly well preserved. Luis and Rosa want to look inside and have joined a guided tour. Carlos can't wait to study the statues, but Hector thinks the monkeys are much more fun.

Can you spot all ten llamas?

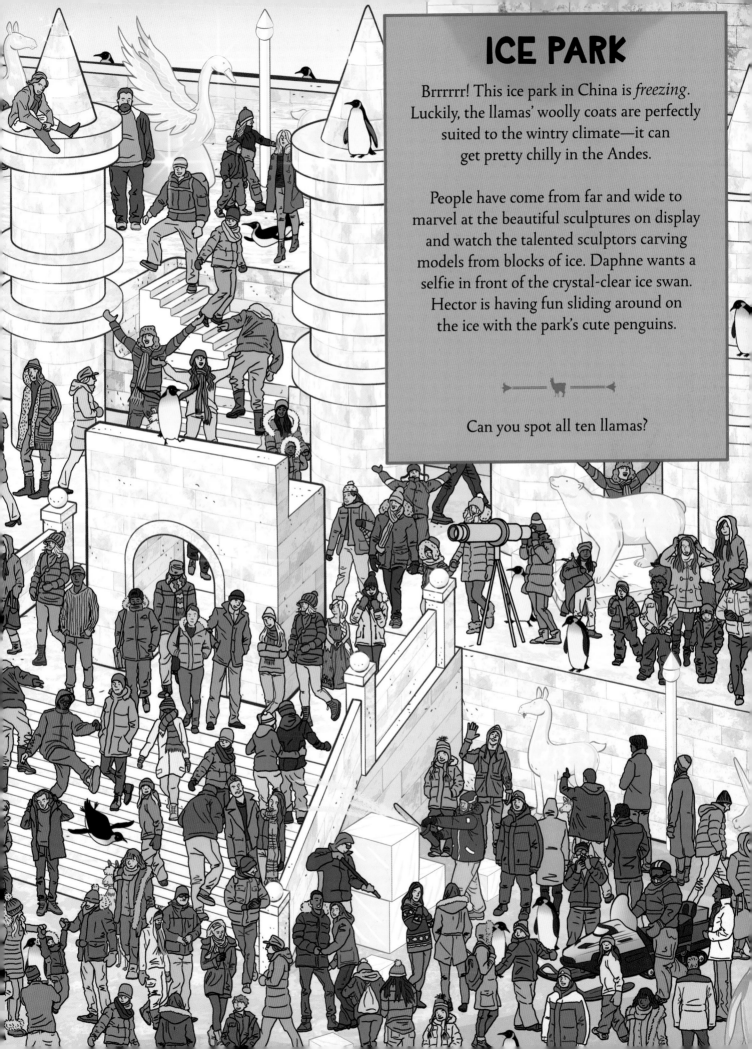

ICE PARK

Brrrrrr! This ice park in China is *freezing*. Luckily, the llamas' woolly coats are perfectly suited to the wintry climate—it can get pretty chilly in the Andes.

People have come from far and wide to marvel at the beautiful sculptures on display and watch the talented sculptors carving models from blocks of ice. Daphne wants a selfie in front of the crystal-clear ice swan. Hector is having fun sliding around on the ice with the park's cute penguins.

Can you spot all ten llamas?

HOT-AIR BALLOON FESTIVAL

Eduardo has arranged to meet some friends at a hot-air balloon festival, and the rest of the herd have decided to join him. Hundreds of balloons have gathered in the sky—it's an incredible sight.

Eduardo can't wait to catch up with his old pals. Carlos and Elena prefer to keep their toes firmly on the ground, but Rosa and Ricardo have persuaded some balloonists to take them for a ride.

Can you spot all ten llamas?

CITY CENTER

The llamas have landed in Melbourne, Australia. They are still getting their heads around the city's complicated tram system but have managed to find their way to its bustling center.

It's lunchtime so Luis is keen to see what the local restaurants have to offer. Daphne can't wait to hit the shops and heads off to enjoy some retail therapy, while Rosa tries to persuade the rest of the herd to join her on a sightseeing tour.

Can you spot all ten llamas?

OLYMPIC GAMES

Nelly can't believe the llamas have got tickets to the Olympics. Although they have arrived early, the stands are already pretty packed, so Beatriz and Eduardo lead the herd into the crowd to find some seats.

But a few of the llamas can't resist getting closer to the action. Nelly's gone to get jumping tips from some world-class athletes, and is that Carlos who's just won a gold medal in the 100 meters?

Can you spot all ten llamas?

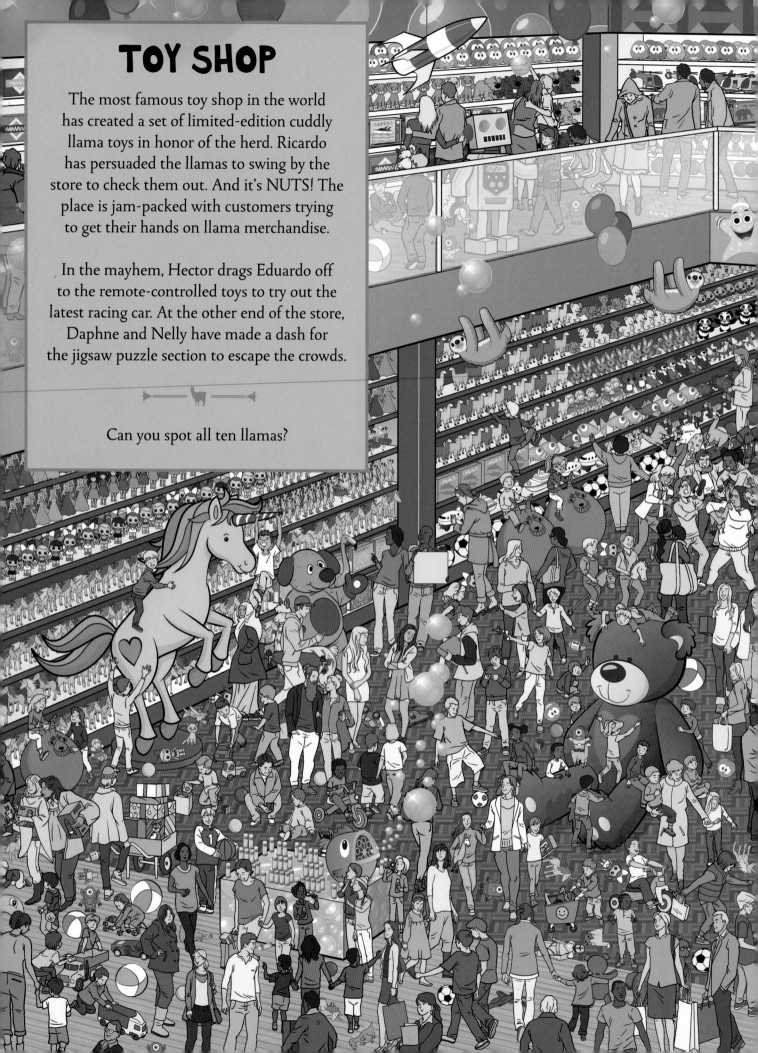

TOY SHOP

The most famous toy shop in the world has created a set of limited-edition cuddly llama toys in honor of the herd. Ricardo has persuaded the llamas to swing by the store to check them out. And it's NUTS! The place is jam-packed with customers trying to get their hands on llama merchandise.

In the mayhem, Hector drags Eduardo off to the remote-controlled toys to try out the latest racing car. At the other end of the store, Daphne and Nelly have made a dash for the jigsaw puzzle section to escape the crowds.

Can you spot all ten llamas?

HOT SPRINGS

After weeks on the road, Beatriz is desperate for some quality "me" time. She's treating the herd to a day at a tranquil hot spring before they head home.

The warm, bubbling water does wonders for the llamas' fleeces. Elena and Daphne want to get mud facials, while Eduardo orders a hot chocolate from the café. Nelly isn't one for sitting still and is having a competition with some kids to see who can make the biggest splash.

Can you spot all ten llamas?

LLAMA LAND

It's time to head back home to Peru—
the llamas can't believe they've come
to the end of their tour already.

They've traveled all around the world,
seen some incredible sights, and met
hundreds of wonderful llama fans. However,
nothing has prepared them for the welcome
they receive in the Andes. Llamas from
all over the country have turned out for
a party to celebrate their return. What a
way to end their llama-zing adventure!

Can you spot all ten llamas?

ANSWERS

SPOTTER'S CHECKLIST

A pickpocket ☐

Someone with binoculars ☐

A boy letting go of his balloon ☐

A small brown dog ☐

A child having their face painted ☐

DAY OF THE DEAD

MIAMI BEACH

SPOTTER'S CHECKLIST

Nine inflatable llamas ☐

A sandcastle that's about to get flooded ☐

A woman wearing a pink hat, pink top, and pink skirt ☐

A swimmer wearing goggles and a green cap ☐

A man wearing orange and green shorts ☐

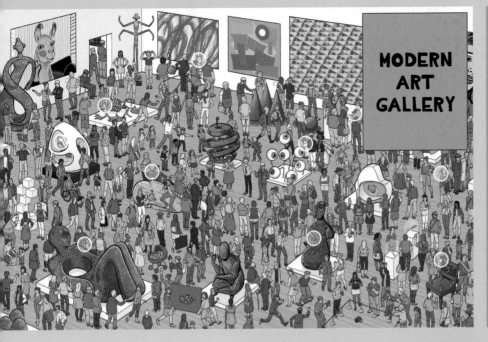

MODERN ART GALLERY

SPOTTER'S CHECKLIST

A man with a cat ☐

A toddler being given a drink ☐

A skateboarder ☐

A man sitting on an artwork eating a sandwich ☐

A child with a teddy bear ☐

FAIRGROUND

SPOTTER'S CHECKLIST

A girl holding a teddy bear ☐

A man with a tire ☐

A man eating chips ☐

A woman with a pink and purple hat ☐

A boy and his dad on the spiral slide ☐

MUSIC FESTIVAL

SPOTTER'S CHECKLIST

A woman with a tambourine ☐

A man dressed in a Tudor costume ☐

A couple dressed in ancient Greek costumes ☐

A man in a cat costume ☐

A flag with a pizza on it ☐

TULIP GARDEN

SPOTTER'S CHECKLIST

A gardener with a wheelbarrow ☐

Three bottles of sunscreen ☐

Three herons ☐

A brown hen ☐

A baby in a yellow sling ☐

SPOTTER'S CHECKLIST

A dog eating a sandwich ☐

A boy in a sweater that's too big for him ☐

A woman spilling her drink ☐

A knight's helmet ☐

A woman smelling a rose ☐

STREET MARKET

FASHION SHOW

SPOTTER'S CHECKLIST

A model who's stepping on another model's dress ☐

A model who's fallen asleep backstage ☐

A runaway dog ☐

A model who can't get her boot off ☐

A man with blue hair and a pink beard ☐

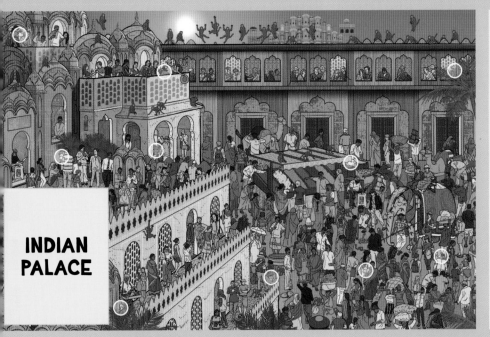

INDIAN PALACE

SPOTTER'S CHECKLIST

A man meditating ☐

An Indiana Jones look-alike ☐

A man with a monkey on his shoulder ☐

A woman wearing a yellow headscarf ☐

A woman carrying bananas on her head ☐

SPOTTER'S CHECKLIST

A family of sun bears ☐

A monkey with a butterfly on its nose ☐

A monkey stealing a sandwich ☐

A tour guide with a red flag ☐

A man dropping a drink can ☐

CAMBODIAN JUNGLE

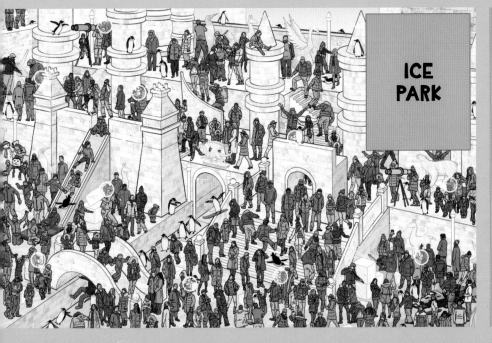

ICE PARK

SPOTTER'S CHECKLIST

A penguin on a snowboard ☐

A dragon sculpture ☐

Two snowmen ☐

A telescope ☐

A snowmobile ☐

HOT-AIR BALLOON FESTIVAL

SPOTTER'S CHECKLIST

A girl with a flower on her backpack ☐

A little boy with a red balloon ☐

A llama-shaped hot-air balloon ☐

A man with a blue and white T-shirt ☐

A plain white hot-air balloon ☐

SPOTTER'S CHECKLIST

A blue hat for sale ☐

A man reading a newspaper ☐

A little girl wearing green shoes and yellow socks ☐

Five rats ☐

A woman with a red headband and red trousers ☐

CITY CENTER

SPOTTER'S CHECKLIST

A viking ☐

A priest ☐

A man wearing a sombrero ☐

An athlete with a broken pole ☐

An athlete wearing a pink baseball cap ☐

OLYMPIC GAMES

TOY SHOP

SPOTTER'S CHECKLIST

A boy on roller skates ☐

A wheelbarrow full of presents ☐

Six hippety-hops ☐

A llama tug-of-war ☐

A panda that's the odd one out ☐

SPOTTER'S CHECKLIST

A man getting a soothing head massage ☐

A girl with a ponytail and water pistol ☐

A boy jumping into the water ☐

Two pink air mattresses ☐

Two Labradors ☐

HOT SPRINGS

LLAMA LAND

SPOTTER'S CHECKLIST

A bell ☐

A music-loving llama ☐

A llama with a pink bow and a gold earring ☐

A red scarf with a yellow stripe ☐

A llama reading a book ☐

Andrews McMeel Publishing
a division of Andrews McMeel Universal
1130 Walnut Street, Kansas City, Missouri 64106
www.andrewsmcmeel.com

First published in Great Britain in 2018 by Michael O'Mara
Books, Ltd. 9 Lion Yard, Tremadoc Road, London SW4 7NQ

19 20 21 22 23 RLP 10 9 8 7 6 5 4 3 2 1

ISBN: 978-1-4494-9729-3

Library of Congress Control Number: 2018952564

Made by:
Shenzhen Reliance Printing Co., Ltd
Address and Location of Manufacturer:
25 Longshan Industrial Zone, Nanling,
Longgang District, Shenzhen, China, 518114
1st printing—11/5/18

Editor: Jean Z. Lucas
Art Director: Holly Swayne
Production Manager: Tamara Haus
Production Editor: Dave Shaw
Designers: Angie Allison and Jack Clucas

ATTENTION: SCHOOLS AND BUSINESSES
Andrews McMeel books are available at quantity discounts
with bulk purchase for educational, business, or sales
promotional use. For information, please e-mail the
Andrews McMeel Publishing Special Sales Department:
specialsales@amuniversal.com.

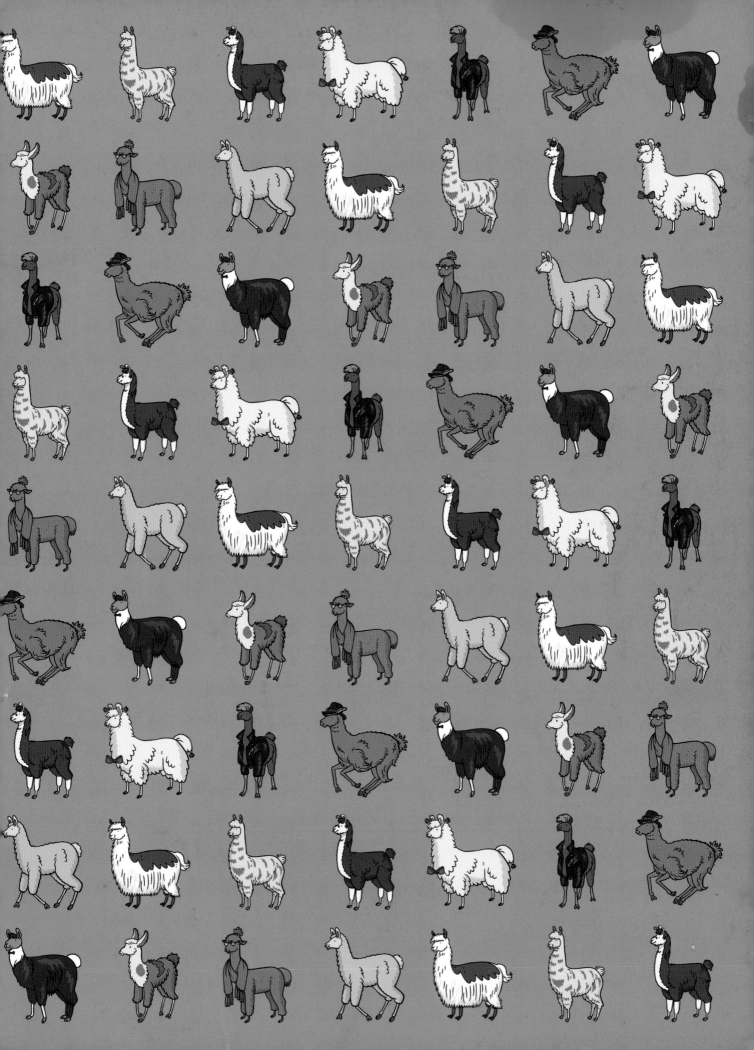